Turkey Tot

by George Shannon

illustrated by
Jennifer K. Mann

Holiday House / New York

To "Turkey Tots" everywhere!
G. S.

To H. and E. and N.—bok bok!
J. K. M.

HOLIDAY HOUSE is registered in the U.S. Patent and Trademark Office.
Printed and Bound in October 2013 at Kwong Fat Offset Printing Co., Ltd., DongGuan City, China.
The text typeface is Oldavai.
The artwork was created with pencil, watercolor, and digital collage.
www.holidayhouse.com
3 5 7 9 10 8 6 4 2

Library of Congress Cataloging-in-Publication Data
Shannon, George.
Turkey Tot / by George Shannon ; illustrated by Jennifer K. Mann. — 1st ed.
p. cm.
ISBN 978-0-8234-2379-8 (hardcover)
[1. When Turkey Tot and his friends spot some fat, juicy blackberries hanging high above their heads, Turkey Tot tries hard to figure out a way to reach them. 2. Determination (Personality trait)—Fiction. 3. Turkeys—Fiction. 4. Animals—Fiction.] I. Mann, Jennifer K., ill. II. Title.
PZ7.S5288Tu 2012
[E]—dc23
2011022103

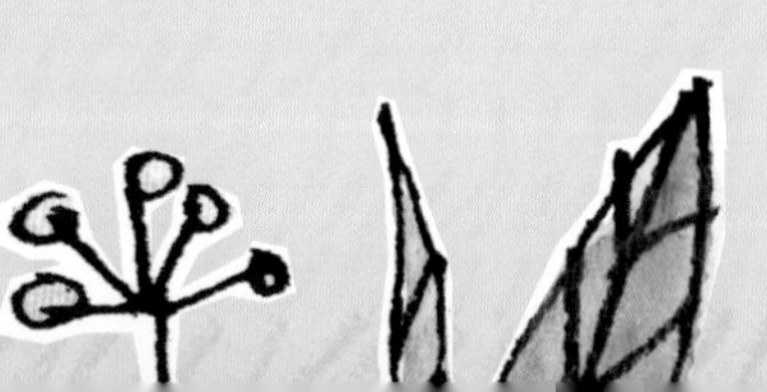

Turkey Tot stared
at the fat blackberries
hanging overhead.

“So juicy and sweet,”
said Chick
with a quiet sigh.

Pig nodded.
"But much too high."

Hen shook her head.
"*Very* high. No sweet and juicy treat today."

All four friends shook their heads
as they walked to the pond.

"Look!" Turkey Tot yelled.
"Good luck. I found
a ball of string!"

"It's not sweet," said Chick.

"Or juicy," said Pig.

"We're hungry," said Hen.
"And we can't eat string."

Turkey Tot grinned.
"But . . . if you help
me find balloons,
we can tie them
to the string.
Then we can float
UP to the berries
for a sweet,
juicy treat."

"Not me," said Chick.
"You're talking silly talk."

"Not me," said Pig.
"We can't reach
the berries, and
that is that."

"*Tsk, tsk,*" said Hen.
"He's been different
since the day
he hatched."

Turkey Tot shrugged.
"Then I'll find some
balloons myself."

But he couldn't.
So he didn't.
But he found
something else.

"Look!" Turkey Tot yelled
as he hurried to his friends.
"More luck. I found a hammer
and nails.

"If we find some sticks,
we can make a ladder.
Then we'll climb UP
to the berries
for a sweet,
juicy treat."

"Not me," said Chick.
"You're talking silly talk."

"Not me," said Pig.
"We can't reach
the berries, and
that is that."

"*Tsk, tsk,*" said Hen.
"He's been different
since the day
he hatched."

Turkey Tot shrugged.
"Then I'll find some
sticks myself."

But he couldn't.
So he didn't.
But he found
something else.

"More luck," he yelled.
"I found a tin can.

"If we find a board,
we can make a
teeter-totter.
Then we'll bounce UP
to the berries
for a sweet,
juicy treat!"

"Not me," said Chick.
"You're talking silly talk."

"Not me," said Pig.
"We can't reach
the berries,
and that is that."

"*Tsk, tsk,*" said Hen.
"He's been different
since the day
he hatched."

Turkey Tot sighed.
"Then I'll go find
a board myself."

But he couldn't.
So he didn't.
But he found
something else.

"Look, look!"
Turkey Tot ran to his friends.
"More luck. I found *another* tin can.
If we—"

“Stop!” said Chick, Pig,
and Hen at once.
“We can’t reach the berries,
and that is THAT!”

Turkey Tot sighed.
“But if you—”

"NO," said Chick.
"You're talking silly talk."

"No," said Pig.
"We're going to the pond
for a nice, long nap."

"*Tsk, tsk,*" said Hen.
"He's been different
since the day he hatched."

Chick, Pig, and Hen were napping
when Chick heard
thunk-a-thunk-a-THUNK. . . .

“Momma,” cried Chick.
“Something’s coming,
and I don’t know—

“PEEEEEEP!”

Pig and Hen jumped awake.
All three stared up at Turkey Tot.

"What's in the basket?" asked Chick.
"And how'd you get so tall?"

Turkey Tot grinned.
"A sweet, juicy treat!"

"But how?" said Pig.

"Two cans made stilts.
Hammer and nails made holes.
And string made handles."

"You're the best!" said Chick.

"Who'd have thought?" said Pig.

"Turkey Tot!" Hen clucked.
"He's been different
since the day he hatched."